For
Elijahsaurus
and
Rachaelodon

My two favourite
cake eating dinosaurs

xxx

There's a story you are told,
when you are very young,
of dinosaurs and what they eat
and where they used to roam.

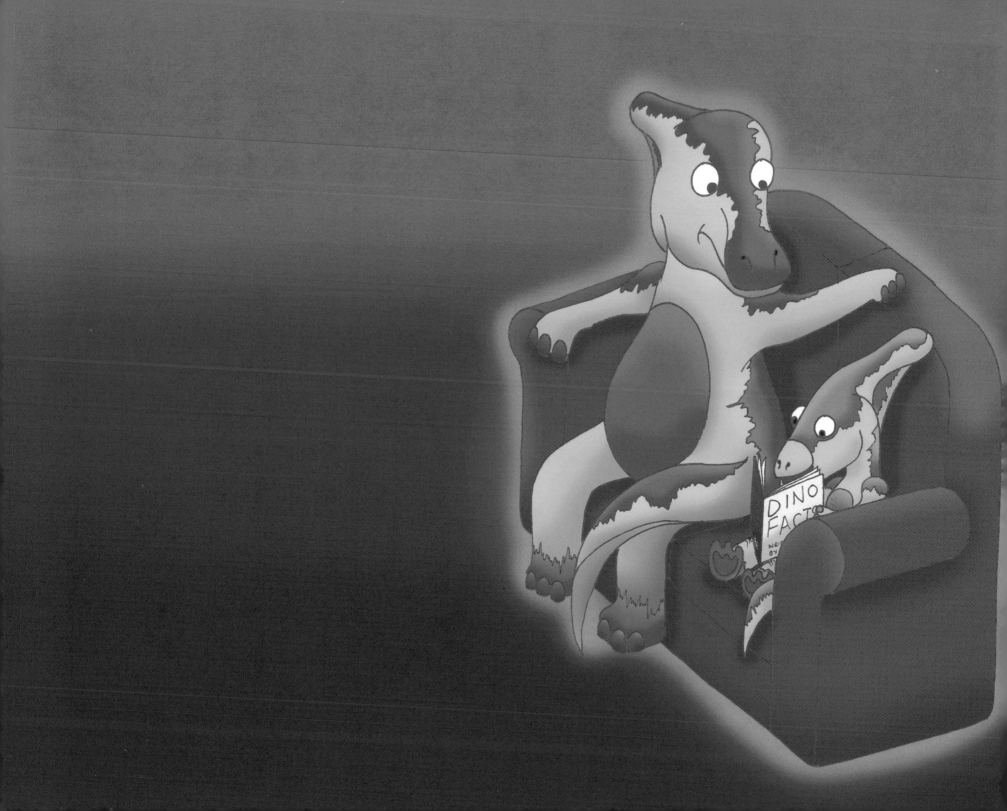

The meat-o-saurs eat meat
and the veg-o-saurs eat veg,
but that's a fib! It's a mistake!
In actual fact, they all eat cake!

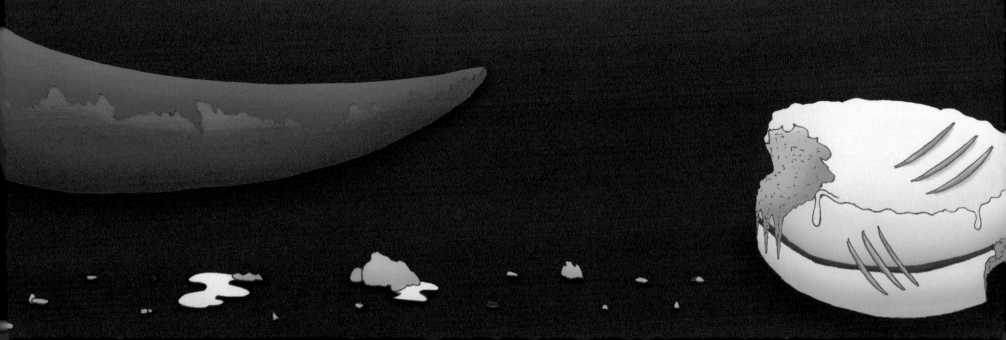

Diplodocus stomps around,
her long neck in the sky.
Every day she loves to eat
a giant pecan pie!

(dih-PLOD-uh-kus)

This is an Iguanodon,
with extra spiky thumbs.
No trace he leaves of carrot cake,
except a load of crumbs!

(ig-WAN-oh-don)

Allosaurus is a grumpy thing.
He really can't be trusted.
I wouldn't interrupt him
while he's eating cake with custard!

(AL-uh-SAWR-us)

Stegosaurus sits around,
those large plates on her back.
Most of all she likes to eat
a golden-brown flapjack!

(STEG-uh-SAWR-us)

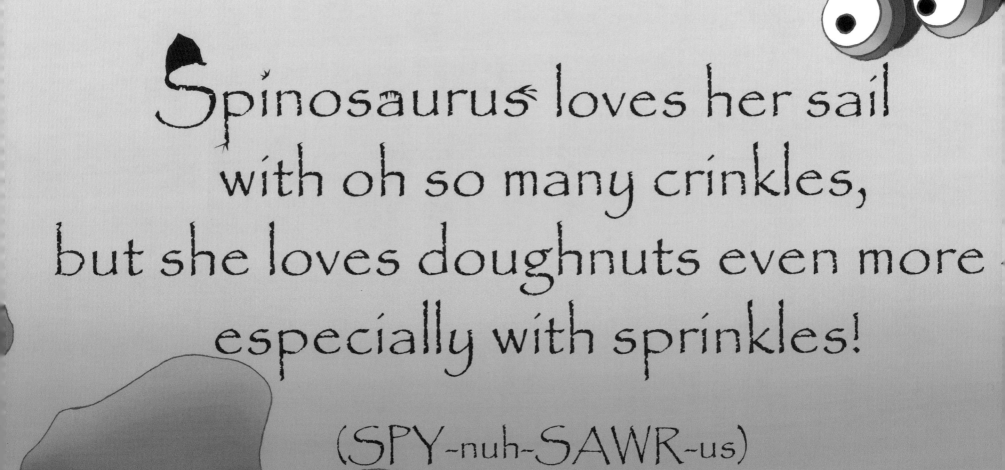

Spinosaurus loves her sail
with oh so many crinkles,
but she loves doughnuts even more
especially with sprinkles!

(SPY-nuh-SAWR-us)

This one has a sail as well.
He's called Dimetrodon.
With lots and lots of jam and cream,
he loves to scoff a scone!

(dye-MEH-truh-don)

Look at Archaeopteryx!
Her feathers shine so bright.
Her treat of choice is rainbow cake.
She eats it at midnight!

(ar-kee-OP-ter-ix)

Wow! It's Brachiosaurus,
one of the largest of them all,
but he loves fondant fancies
as they're really, really small!

(BRACK-ee-uh-SAWR-us)

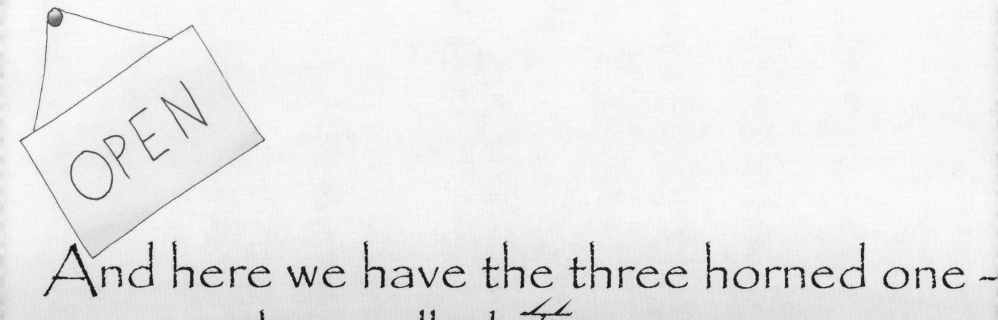

And here we have the three horned one –
she's called Triceratops.
Too posh to eat a homemade cake,
she buys hers from the shops!

(try-SAIR-uh-tops)

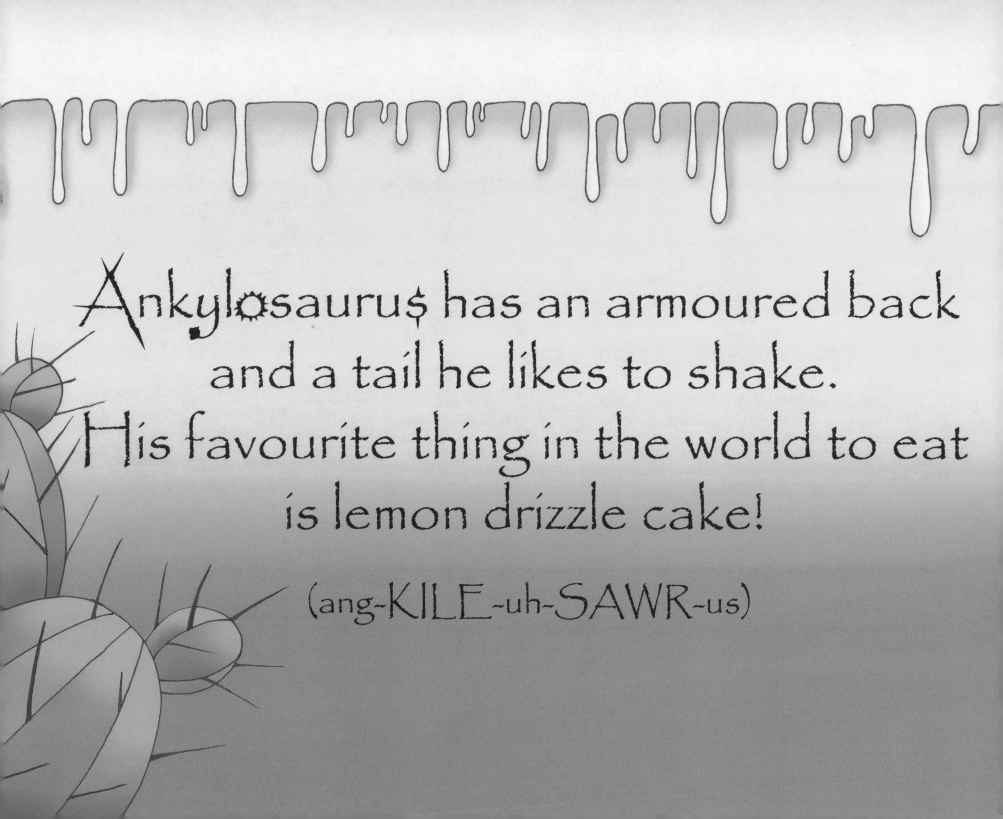

Ankylosaurus has an armoured back
and a tail he likes to shake.
His favourite thing in the world to eat
is lemon drizzle cake!

(ang-KILE-uh-SAWR-us)

Dive and meet the Plesiosaur.
He lives deep in the sea
and couldn't go a day without
a fish-cake for his tea!

(PLEE-see-uh-saw)

Velociraptor speeds around with long claws on his feet. He loves a bun with icing on that's oh so sickly sweet!

(veh-loss-ih-RAP-tor)

And finally, Tyrannosaur,
the king of dinos all.
He only ever eats chocolate cake
that's seven layers tall!

(tye-RAN-uh-SAW)

This book cannot be poured, stirred, mixed, baked or eaten. No dinosaurs were
harmed during the making of this book, although many cakes were tested!

Dinosaurs enjoy cake as part of a varied diet and healthy lifestyle, which includes
getting plenty of exercise!
The Tyrannosaur however has servants to do everything for him
while he stuffs his face, watches TV and never goes outside.
I have no idea how he manages to eat so much chocolate cake and watch
The Great Jurassic Bake Off on repeat with a kingdom to rule!
The Tyrannosaur is silly... Please don't be like the Rex!